A MURKY CASE OF MURDER AT THE MOVIES

AN EMILY CHERRY COZY MYSTERY
BOOK NINE

DONNA DOYLE

PUREREAD.COM

CONTENTS

DEAR READER, GET READY FOR ANOTHER GREAT COZY...

READY TO SOLVE THE MYSTERY?

Turn the page and let's begin

∼

1

"Well, what did you think?" Emily asked as they emerged from the theater and into the lobby of the cinema, blinking at the surprisingly bright lights after being ensconced in darkness for the last two hours. There was something about seeing a movie that had always held a special place in her heart. Maybe it was the glitz and glamor of big film stars, maybe it was the lush old-fashioned décor of the cinema, or maybe it was just all the delicious junk food, but she loved it all the same.

Anita took the last bite of her popcorn and dropped the bag in the trash can. "I think it was a lot better than the book, but don't let anyone else catch me saying that. You know everyone always says the book is better. I don't think that's always true. Then again, sometimes I'm too lazy to actually read the book.

"You don't really ever read these days, do you?" Emily asked with a smile, knowing that even when they were out shopping and they stopped at Alexandria's Books, Anita only went as a kindness to her. She usually found a magazine to flip through, but she didn't dive into stories the way Emily did.

"No, this was a rare exception," her best friend admitted. "I do think they should've cast the part of Spencer differently. I don't think anyone that good looking could possibly be that romantic."

Emily laughed. "Does that mean this movie should've been categorized as a fantasy instead of a romance?"

"Oh, definitely! The only other thing I would change was that obnoxious man two rows ahead of us. He kept turning on his cell phone screen and muttering to himself. I've half a mind to say something to him, although I suppose I should've had him kicked out before he ruined the whole movie." Anita shook her head, making her bright red earrings swish back and forth as they headed into the restroom. "I need to fix my hair. I'm sure it got crushed against the seat."

"You know, coming here today has made me think that perhaps I ought to do some movie reviews on my blog." Emily had been thinking it the entire time they'd been watching the movie.

"Instead of the book blogs?" Anita asked.

"No, I think they would actually serve as nice companion pieces." Emily leaned over the counter to look in the big mirror. Her wild red hair had more and more streaks of gray through it these days, but she'd learned to accept that. It made it a little easier to find a shade of lipstick that looked decent on her. She fluffed out the back of it, but it didn't seem to be affected much by their time in the theater. "We were just talking about how people like to compare the movie and the book, so I could offer reviews on both. I think it could be fun, and it would offer some variety."

Anita gave Emily's reflection an approving nod. "Then you should do it! I think people might really like it. Oh, by the way. Did you know the girl at the concession counter? She looked familiar." Taking a comb out of her purse, Anita carefully straightened out her short hair.

To Emily, it looked completely fine as it was. "Yes, that was Zoe Poole. She used to work at the antique store, and her brother had been the culprit in one of my very first accidental investigations. She works here now, and I was surprised she remembered me."

"Don't be silly. You're very memorable." Anita added an extra layer of lipstick.

"Is it the hair?" Emily asked with a grin.

"That's certainly part of it," Anita retorted. They stepped back out into the lobby, and she pointed at a man who had just come out of the same theater they'd left. "Look, there's that annoying man I was just speaking about a minute ago."

The man in question had just emerged from the theater. He was short and squat with a balding head and glasses that continually slipped down his nose. Pushing these up with one finger, he walked over to the assistant manager, who stood in the corner of the lobby near his office. "I'll be sure to let you know as soon as I get the review posted so you can share it on your own social media."

The assistant manager was a young man by the name of Mason. Emily knew him from her volunteer work at the shelter, when he'd offered to take custody of his deceased roommate's dog Diesel. Mason ran a hand through his shaggy dark hair. "Thanks, Walter. I'll be sure to keep an eye out."

"Any time, any time!" Walter enthused, rolling his hand through the air. "I know my reviews only help your place here. Free advertising! But you don't have to thank me for it. I do my best to give back to the community when I can."

Mason nodded, clearly doing his best to keep his patience. "Thanks again, Walter. I guess we'll probably see you later this week?"

"Of course! I wouldn't miss it for the world! The premier of the long-awaited *Defenders of Fortune!* More people have been focused on the cast, the director, and the budget than anything else, but it was actually based on a book from some years ago. Did you know that?" Walter looked up at Mason over his glasses as though this were some sort of challenge.

"I think I might've heard that." Mason watched the lobby, looking for any excuse not to talk to the man.

"I guess he's just as irritating outside the movies as he is during one," Anita commented with a giggle.

After a minute filled with more promises of excellent reviews and free advertising for the theater, Walter left. Emily wandered over to say hi. "Hello, Mason. How is Diesel doing these days?"

"Emily! It's nice to see you. I'm sure Diesel would think so, too, if he were here." Mason smiled, looking much more relaxed to be speaking with her instead of to Walter.

She chuckled at that, remembering how the dog had been leery of everyone during his short stint in the shelter. Emily was the only person he liked, and she found that she liked him as well. "I'm sure he would."

"He's actually getting a lot better around strangers. I've been working with him, slowly getting him used to people I know personally and then taking him out in public. He's calmed down a lot, so we've made some great progress."

"I'm so glad," Emily replied genuinely. She'd been volunteering at Best Friends Furever for a while now, and she truly got attached to the animals who came to stay there. "I have a question for you. Is that man you were just speaking with an actual movie critic? I didn't think there were any around here."

Mason shrugged. "Not exactly. He does reviews for his blog. He's got a bit of a following, I guess. He didn't bother you, did he?"

"Not unless I was trying to watch the movie," Anita commented.

"I'm sorry about that." Mason sighed as he ran his hand through his hair again. "We've had some complaints about him before, but every time we threaten to kick him out he says he's going to talk to the owner. I called his bluff on that once, and it turns out he actually *knows* the owner. My hands are tied. Meanwhile, he acts like he's doing us some great favor by doing his movie reviews from here instead of somewhere else. There's a small mention of our cinema, but I don't think it actually makes a difference in how many tickets we sell."

"You must be talking about Walter Powell," Zoe said as she walked over. The concession counter was empty for the moment, as the next round of films hadn't yet started. She rolled her eyes and shook her head. "I always hope that I won't be working when he comes in, but since he's in here all the time, there's no avoiding him."

"Not that we don't like our regulars," Mason added quickly. "We've got movie buffs who never miss a premier. Like that lady right over there. She's here at least once a week, sometimes even twice. Zoe, looks like you're on deck."

Zoe trotted over to help the woman Mason had indicated. She had blonde wavy hair down to her shoulders with thick bangs, and her bright yellow blouse stood out amongst the dark red décor of the cinema.

"There are others, too," Mason went on to explain. "We've got entire families who make the movies their traditional way of celebrating. I guess that's why a guy like Walter bothers me so much. People really take their film experience to heart sometimes, but he wants to hog it all for himself."

One such family filed by them at the moment, two parents followed by three children. The middle child had a pink crown on that said, 'Birthday Girl.'

"Excuse me. I'll have to talk to you ladies later." Mason headed over to check tickets as more customers began to flood in.

"Maybe I'm wrong about doing the movie reviews," Emily mused as they headed outside onto the pavement. The world felt very real compared to the fictional experience they'd just had.

"Why would you say that?" The air was beginning to chill as summer came to an end, and Anita buttoned up her jacket.

"Well, there are two reasons. One is that Walter Powell already has a blog dedicated to movie reviews. He might be a pain, but he must know what he's doing. That's quite a bit of competition." Emily frowned as she thought about it.

Anita let out a short laugh. "As though that's ever stopped you before! There are any number of blogs and websites and books about all of the topics you've covered. The world is big enough for everyone's voice, I think."

Emily smiled. "That's a very nice way of putting it, and I'd like to think you're right."

"So what's the other problem?" Anita pressed. They reached her car and climbed inside.

"You heard what Mason said about how much people take their movie experience to heart. For some, a review might be nothing more than a tool to help them decide if they want to see a particular film. But for others, it's much more than that. I wouldn't want anything I write to impact someone so much that it changes their whole experience of things."

"But isn't that exactly what you're doing every time you write?" Anita pointed out as she turned over the engine. "I don't mean that in a bad way, either. Emily, you're an excellent writer. Even when you're writing about something as simple as a cute thing Rosemary did, you do a wonderful job. I don't think you have anything to worry about, and you absolutely need to do these movie reviews."

"You really think so?"

"I do," Anita confirmed as she pulled out onto the street. "You've proven yourself to be an excellent blogger over the last few years. It was nothing I'd ever even given a thought to, and you hardly knew a thing about it yourself. But here you are, carving out your little space in the world. I wouldn't want you to give that up, or even to give up a part of it that you're interested in."

Emily smiled. "You're a dear friend. You know that?"

"Yes, I do," she replied with a smile.

As they headed through Little Oakley, Emily began to think on just how she would do her reviews.

2

"Emily, it's nice to see you again," Mason said as he checked her ticket. "Going for the big action movie today, hm? It's a great one."

"I thought it would be a nice change from the romance that my friend and I came to see the other day," she replied. She wavered a moment and then decided to go ahead and tell him. "You know, I was thinking about starting up my own movie reviews on my blog."

"Really? That's wonderful to hear." Mason looked genuinely pleased. "It'll be interesting to see how your views differ from Walter's."

"I hadn't really thought about it like that," she admitted.

"I'm sorry to say it, but he's in the same theater you are," he said quietly as he handed over her ticket stub. "He just came through a few minutes ago. There's not much I can do, but feel free to come and get me anyway if he gets to be too bothersome."

"I will." But Emily had a feeling that she probably wouldn't do any such thing. She wasn't the kind of person who got others kicked out of a movie theater or complained to the management. Instead, she was determined to have her own experience and report on it to her readers.

The line for the concession counter was a long one, but that was just as well. Emily passed it by and went straight to her seat. She wouldn't be using her time to munch on popcorn or drink a regrettable amount of soda. She hadn't even brought Anita along so they could look at the handsome actors or gasp over the amount of violence.

Instead, she vowed to herself as she walked down the aisle to look for her seat, she would be paying attention to the plot and characters arcs. She would think about the special effects and if they were done well enough to serve the movie. She would decide whether or not the actors had been cast well. And though it went against her nature to do so on most things, she would be the judge of whether or not the director and producers should've done something differently.

When the opening credits began, Emily felt that familiar thrill of excitement in her chest that she always got when she came to see a film in the theater. She smiled and took out her small pad of paper and a pen, wanting to jot that down so she'd be sure to include it at the beginning of her post. Unfortunately, even the bright white paper was difficult to see in this light. She scribbled something out, but she doubted she'd be able to read it later.

Walter, however, was having no trouble at all. He was also making notes already, and he was doing so on his cell phone. The screen lit up like a beacon down in the front few rows of the theater, much to the disgust of the moviegoers around him. Several whispered to each other, and someone even tossed a few pieces of popcorn his way, but Walter was completely oblivious to any of this judgment. He was too focused on the movie. It was ironic that he was ruining the very movie experience that he was trying to review for others.

Ignoring him, Emily returned her focus to the screen. An action movie might not have been the best first choice, she realized. How was she to criticize it when she was used to watching romance and drama? She couldn't compare it to very many other films. Steeling herself and taking a deep breath, she reminded herself that this was only the first of many. It was the beginning, and things were never perfect in the beginning. Her readers had forgiven her time and again for changing topics or adding new ones. If they came to her site for a book review and found one about a movie, they would either read it and appreciate it or they would ignore it altogether.

About halfway through, just as the bad guys were gaining ground and it seemed that all hope might be lost for the hero, Emily's throat began to get dry. She swallowed and decided she would treat herself afterwards. But the more she tried to ignore her thirst, the more obnoxious it became, much like Walter down there tapping gleefully away on his phone.

Guilt stabbed through her as she stood up and made her way out to the concession. She hated to miss any part of a movie that she'd be analyzing for others, but she wasn't going to remember a single thing about it other than how thirsty she was. Smiling, she thought that might actually serve as an amusing comment within her post.

The movie soundtrack made a dull roar in the lobby, even through the closed double doors. There was no line at the concession counter, nor was there anyone behind it. Emily stepped up and waited for a moment, inhaling the salty scent of the popcorn. Hot dogs sat under a warming light. Those weren't supposed to be a part of her diet, considering she ought to be thinking about heart health and cholesterol these days, but their thick, greasy smell was tempting. If only there was someone here to help her get it. She glanced over toward Mason's office, which was just off the lobby. She could see him through the window in the door, but he was with someone.

"Sorry!" Zoe panted as she came running out of the restroom and zoomed in behind the counter. She quickly washed her hands at the small sink. "I'm trying to keep up with a bit of everything right now, and someone decided to spill their popcorn all over the restroom floor. Mason doesn't have to do much of any of that since he's the assistant manager, but he's got a customer complaint to deal with right now."

Emily glanced through his window again. "I can't imagine what anyone would have to complain about here. The place is always clean, and you have wonderful service." That got her thinking that perhaps she should write a review not just about the movie she was seeing, but about the cinema itself. Walter claimed that he was giving them some free advertising, but Emily thought she could do her share of that, as well.

"I'm sure it's about Walter again," Zoe said with a shrug. "Mason will just refund their tickets and hope they come back on a day when Walter isn't here. What can I get for you?"

Just as Emily was about to order, a massive banging sound ricocheted through the building. Emily jumped, looking around for the source and wondering if her life was threatened. "What was that?"

Zoe shrugged. "Just the big gunfight scene in the movie."

"Oh, are you sure?" That bothered her both because it sounded so real and because it meant she was probably missing a big part of the movie that her readers would want to know about. Perhaps that was why some of these movie buffs came back to see a film more than once. You didn't always get everything out of it the first time, especially if you had to get up and get a drink.

"Definitely. It's a new film, but it's already played several times. When you've worked here for a while, you get used to those kinds of noises, as well as the timing of them. It's sort of like people who live next to the railway. They know what time the train comes through, so they hardly even hear it."

"Yes, I suppose that's true," Emily had to agree, even though there was still some adrenaline rushing through her bloodstream. "I'll take a small Coke, please."

Soon enough, Emily was back in her seat. She glanced down at Walter, wondering what he'd seen that she'd missed by taking her little trek out to the lobby. She could no longer see the brilliant light from his cell phone and wondered if his fellow watchers had convinced him to turn it off. Her thirst assuaged, she tried to put all of her focus on the movie.

Soon enough, the end credits began to roll. The first set of lights came on, the dimmer ones that illuminated the aisleways for those who wanted to duck out onto the streets before the crowd emerged as a whole. Emily remained in her seat, thinking this would be the perfect time to go ahead and make some of the notes that she'd thought of while watching. She wanted to get them down before she forgot them.

"Excuse me," a gentleman said to her left.

"Oh. I'm sorry." She was nearest the aisle, and so her only option was either to fold up her legs and let everyone pass or to go ahead and leave.

Back in the lobby, Emily already felt herself getting a little more distant from the movie. She didn't want to let go of the thoughts and feelings that it'd put in her mind. This was exactly why she made notes about the books she was reviewing as she read them. It was too easy to forget all the details later. There was plenty of comfortable seating in the lobby, but she didn't want to be out among the crowds. Instead, she looked for a place where she could take her notes in private.

Just around the corner from the restroom, Emily noticed a small alcove. It was near the supply closet, but she didn't think Mason or Zoe would mind if she just settled in over there for a few minutes. Getting her notepad and pen out of her pocket, Emily turned the corner.

There was no place to sit here, but that was all right. It wouldn't take her very long, and her notepad was a small one that fit in the palm of her hand. She leaned against the wall of the alcove and laughed at the bit of scribbling she'd attempted in the dark. Flipping the page, Emily jotted down her thoughts. The acting was well done, even if the characters' abilities seemed a bit overexaggerated. The story itself was tied up neatly at the end while still leaving a little bit of room for a possible sequel, which she liked.

A thump sounded nearby. Emily looked up, but she didn't see anyone or anything. Realizing it was probably just another movie soundtrack, she continued her notes.

She couldn't remember what she'd seen the main actor in before, and Emily reminded herself to look that up when she got home. The actress was very well known, someone who reminded her quite a bit of Anita.

The latch on the supply closet door clicked. Emily looked up once again, ready to apologize to whatever employee emerged. She didn't think it would be a problem to be here, nor had she realized anyone would be in there. She fixed a pleasant smile on her face, but it quickly disappeared as Walter Powell's body sagged through the opening and onto the floor.

3

Mason looked pale when he shut the office door behind him. He swallowed as he came around to take his chair behind his desk. "The police confirmed it was a gunshot wound. I just don't know how this could've happened. Emily, are you sure you're all right?"

"I know the police don't really want us out there, but I'm sure they'd let me get behind the concession counter to get you a drink or something," Zoe offered.

Emily waved away their concerns. They'd been hovering over her ever since she'd come to tell them what she'd found. She couldn't really blame them, knowing that she'd probably looked incredibly frightened at the time. And, of course, she had been. This certainly wasn't the first time she'd seen a dead body, and it wasn't even the first time she'd stumbled across one, but that didn't mean that it really got any easier.

"I'm all right," she assured them. Though she was a bit shaken, she was more concerned with figuring out who did this. She looked through the window in Mason's office door. The customers had all been cleared out of the cinema, leaving only the two employees and herself. The police now swarmed through the building, looking for any evidence. "You said there are security cameras?"

"Only a few," Mason said with a shrug. "I gave the police access to them, but I don't think they'll help very much. We're set up more to check for people who try to sneak into the cinema without buying a ticket than anything else."

Right now, a free movie hardly seemed like a crime at all. She toyed with her cell phone in her purse, but she already knew it wouldn't do any good to contact Alyssa. The young detective constable that she'd befriended was out of town on vacation at the moment. It didn't seem fair to bother her with police business when the girl would be swimming in it once she returned.

"Using a gun in a public place is pretty bold," Mason mused, fiddling with a pencil on his desk. "How could you be certain that nobody would hear it?"

Zoe had the answer right away. "They had to have timed it out with the gunfight scene in the movie. It's incredibly loud. I don't think you'd hear anything over that."

Emily wasn't entirely certain that she *hadn't* heard it. The sound she'd heard while standing at the concession counter had been deafening. She'd been reassured by Zoe's explanation in the moment, but now she had to wonder.

Mason nodded. "So it was someone who knew the movie well enough, even though it's a fairly new one, to get the timing down."

"Right," Zoe confirmed.

A deep silence fell over the office as the three of them contemplated the possibilities.

"Hold on," Zoe said suddenly, sitting up straight in her chair. She looked at Mason with wide eyes.

His mouth was a hard line as he nodded. "I don't like what you're thinking, but I agree. The two of us are the prime suspects right now. We know these movies better than anyone else."

Zoe brought her ponytail over her shoulder and ran her hands down it repetitively as she pulled her feet up into her chair. She was a young woman, but she looked like a little girl just then. "I'd never hurt anyone! All I do is scoop out popcorn, sweep the floors, and tell everyone to have a nice day when they leave!"

Mason's hand riffled through his hair. "I got caught shoplifting when I was thirteen. It's on my juvenile record, and I think that's supposed to be sealed or something, but

I sure hope it doesn't make them come back and think I did this."

"Don't forget how much we've been ragging on Walter lately," Zoe groaned. "We see him all the time. We know his habits and his schedules. We're the absolute prime targets here!"

The panic was building up so much in the room that it was nearly palpable. "Just hold on," Emily said calmly. "You both know the cinema and the movies quite well, that much I can agree on. Neither one of you were Walter's biggest fans, and that's certainly a factor. But I'm your primary witness to the fact that neither of you had anything to do with this."

They both looked at her quickly. "What do you mean?" Mason asked.

"If the murder happened during the gunfight scene in the movie, which we're fairly certain it did," Emily postulated, "then you were both otherwise occupied. Zoe, you were behind the concession counter, chatting with me while I ordered a Coke. Mason, I saw you where you're sitting right now, here in your office with an unhappy customer."

"Oh." Zoe stopped playing with her hair and took a deep breath. "You're right. I completely forgot about that. I really have gotten so used to all the big noises from the theater that they all blend together."

Mason nodded his agreement, his shoulders sagging a little with relief. "You're right. There's never really one time or another that stands out. Funny enough, those customers were complaining about Walter."

Emily already knew that, which led her to the next point she wanted to make. "The two of you are innocent. I'm quite sure of that. This also means that you, Zoe, know that I'm innocent. However, the two of you know this place and its people better than anyone else. Who might've had the motivation to kill Walter?"

Mason leaned back in his chair and put his hands behind his head. "That could turn into a very long list. People complain about him regularly."

"What about the person who owns this cinema?" Emily pressed. "You said Walter was friends with him and wouldn't have him thrown out. Perhaps he was getting upset about all of the complaints, and he thought the only way to deal with the problem was to get rid of it entirely."

The assistant manager shook his head. "I can see where you're going with that, but I don't think so. The owner is currently at some big film festival over in New York. He's been sending out all sorts of emails about it, including a news clip."

"Ah, I see." Well, that eliminated one more person right off the bat, but it didn't make Emily want to give up. "There must be someone else."

"I actually have an entire folder on the people who've complained about Walter," Mason admitted. "I was putting it together with the hope that I could take it to my manager, and then he might bring it up to the owner. I thought if there was enough evidence against him, they might finally do something about it. I'll give it to the police and let them look through it."

"Good," Emily said with a firm nod. "That's a very good start. They might even be able to check that information against any other information they have. Anything else that might be relevant?"

Silence descended once again. Emily wondered why it felt so eerily quiet, when she remembered that all of the movies had been shut down while the building was being evacuated. There was no deep rumbling or wild laughter emanating from the theaters around them. It was a strange feeling, and one that she wasn't sure she liked.

Zoe shifted uncomfortably in her seat. "I hate that they're making us hole up here and wait. As many officers as there are in the building right now, you'd think they could spare one to come and start the questioning. I'd rather get it over with while things are fresh in my mind. I'm already feeling like I've thought about it too much."

"They'll get to us when they do," Mason replied. He was trying to sound calm, but Emily could hear the tension in his voice.

"It'll be all right. They know what they're doing," Emily assured them. She just wished that Alyssa was in town and could be on the case. The rest of the Little Oakley Police Department would do just fine, she was sure, but they had no idea just how much Alyssa did to solve their cases. For that matter, they had no idea how much Emily did to help solve their cases, but she'd leave it that way.

Restless, Zoe got up out of her seat and paced the floor. "You know, it's kind of funny. I took this job because I thought it would be safer than working in a shop. You know, in terms of robberies and such. Now I'm not so sure. I know whoever did this didn't turn around and come after us, but still."

"I'm sure this is a very rare thing," Mason replied quietly.

Emily sat back and considered that for a moment. She'd encountered quite a few strange incidents over the last few years. People killed for all sorts of reasons, it seemed, and they weren't ones that were always obvious to everyone else. Though it was never really her business, she liked to do her best to get to the truth so that the criminals could get the justice they deserved. That was the nice, happily-ever-after type of ending that she always wanted to see in a movie, but life wasn't always like the movies. What if, this time, she didn't figure it out?

"You know," Zoe mused. "There was that one filmmaker. Oh, what was his name? The independent guy who managed to get his movie shown here?"

"Elliot Byrne," Mason replied almost instantly. "How could I forget him? He was a very dramatic fellow. He kept trying to get me to adjust the lighting in the theater, because he said it affected how people saw his film."

"Yes, that's the one." Zoe snapped her fingers. "It was a huge deal for him to be shown in a regular cinema. I guess a lot of the independent films are only at festivals, and then they go straight to television. And that's if they're lucky. Do you remember the scathing review Walter gave him?"

Mason nodded. "Tore him to pieces. He said the writing was terrible, the acting was worse, and that the whole film ought to be burned to save anyone else the misery of having to see it."

Emily was a bit blown away by this. "Was Walter always that mean?"

"If he thought he had even the slightest reason to be," Mason confirmed. "Not that he wouldn't praise a movie occasionally, but for the most part he was more interested in pointing out what was wrong with it. Of course, if you're going to start thinking of everyone Walter insulted with his reviews, then you might find an even longer list than those customers who complained about him."

Emily didn't doubt that was true considering everything else she knew about Walter. Still, she thought that might be a very good place to start looking.

4

"Is this the place?" Anita leaned forward to look through the windshield. "It doesn't exactly look like a movie set to me."

Emily put her car in park and double-checked the address. "As far as I can tell, yes."

"How did you find out where he was shooting his latest film, anyway?" Anita pulled down the visor to look in the mirror and adjust her hair. "I thought directors were always private about that sort of thing because they don't want strangers wandering onto the set. You know, like us."

"I don't think he's very private at all, considering how much he posts online. Genevieve knew who I was talking about as soon as I mentioned him. I guess she's a big fan. Anyway, she was able to pull up his social media accounts in no time. He'd written all about his new movie, and he'd even included where he was shooting." Her daughter-in-law had proven to be extremely helpful anytime Emily needed to find information online about someone. Genevieve was in the fashion industry, and she seemed to have her finger on the pulse of anything that was happening.

The two of them got out of the car. The sign over the door denoted the place as simply called Frank's. Inside, they found a small and shabby diner. Several people were seated in the booths, enjoying a meal. A man behind the counter, presumably Frank himself, poked at the cash register as he took orders. Through a pass-through, Emily could see a few folks working in the kitchen. Everything looked perfectly normal except for the cameras set up on tripods here and there. A man stood behind one of them, frowning as he watched a replay of something on one of the cameras.

A young woman in a headset stopped them at the door. "Are you here as extras or to dine?"

"You mean, we can do either?" Emily asked, stunned. Though the filming information had been put up online, she fully expected for there to be something that would stop them from actually getting onto the set.

"Yes," the young woman replied with a nod, "but you'll probably still end up as an extra even if you're just here to dine."

"I'd like to be an extra, please," Anita announced.

"Oh, I don't know about that." Emily touched her wild hair, knowing immediately that she wouldn't be the sort of woman they'd want to put in the background. Extras weren't supposed to be noticeable.

"It's fine," Anita assured her. "You do your thing, and I'll get my name in the credits. Where should I go, dear?" She directed this last question to the woman with the headset.

"Right over there to the counter," she explained. "If we have any lines for you, someone will let you know."

"And to think, I didn't even do my vocal exercises before we came! You let me know if you need me!" Anita whisked off to the counter, where she parked herself on a stool next to several other extras.

"If you're dining, you can have a seat at one of the tables," the woman told Emily. "We may end up seating someone else with you, since we've been very busy today."

"I would imagine so." Emily wondered just how many of these people were here only for food and how many of them had come because they wanted a chance to be in a movie. "I'm actually here because I was hoping to get an interview with Elliot Byrne. I'd like to do an article about him."

"An article?" The woman's eyebrows shot up. "For what paper?"

Emily hadn't even thought about using a newspaper as an excuse, and that would probably be far more appealing.

Since she'd been asked directly, though, she couldn't very well lie. "It's for my blog, actually. I specialize in book and movie reviews." That was a little bit of a stretch, since she hadn't even posted her first movie review yet, but it was still what she planned to do.

"Hold on just a moment." The woman trotted over to the man behind the camera. She stood close as she spoke with him, pointing back at Emily.

Emily tried not to stare at them hopefully, but there wasn't much other place to look. If this didn't work, she'd have to find some other way to see whether or not Mr. Byrne had enough of a vendetta against Walter Powell to kill him.

"He says he'll speak with you as soon as he's done with the next scene," the woman said when she came back. "Have a seat at that table right over there for now."

"Thank you." Hope filled her as she went where she was told. There was a chance she could catch the man red-handed and get Walter's murder solved before the police even had a chance to look through Mason's folder of complaints. If not, then she'd have a fascinating article she could post on her blog. She couldn't lose, and Anita looked more than happy to be serving as an extra.

After another look at the camera, Mr. Byrne straightened. He wore a white button-down shirt that had become partially untucked. His steely gray hair was cut so that it was about three inches long all over. Either he was used to running his hands through it all the time or he took care to style it to make it look as though he did. He adjusted his glasses on his nose as he looked around the diner. "All right, people. We're going to shoot the next scene. Johnathan comes in and sits down right over here, and he interacts with the waitress. Just like the last one. Eat your meals, have some casual conversation with whoever is next to you. I'm not worried about noise. Just don't get between this camera and the table. Action!"

Emily watched as a young man entered the café and sat down. She could only catch bits and pieces of his conversation with the waitress. With the normal diner noises all around her, she'd never have any idea that something was being filmed here if it weren't for the cameras, the director, and his assistant. That seemed to her as though it would make a scene look very realistic, and she wondered just what Walter hadn't liked about his last movie.

When it was all over with and Mr. Byrne had watched the replay on his camera, he strode over and flopped into the booth across from her. "Elliot Byrne."

"Emily Cherry." He didn't extend his hand, and so neither did she. "I truly appreciate you taking the time to speak with me."

"Yes, well. I'm not sure I should, considering what that other blogger wrote." He made an irritated noise and squinted out the window into the sunshine.

"What other blogger would that be?" she asked innocently.

"Walter Powell," came the instant reply. "I was lucky enough to get my last film, *Moon over Pavement*, shown in a local cinema. Walter made this big deal out of reviewing it. I was foolish enough to think he could truly help get the word out about my films. I mean, he was a legitimate movie reviewer for the paper before he'd launched his own website."

"I can see why that would make a difference for you." It sounded as though Emily was lucky indeed that Elliot was even speaking to her. She had no idea that Walter had worked for the paper before. That was something she would have to look into later. There would be archived editions available, she was sure.

"Then, as I'm sure you know if you've done any research on me at all, he proceeded to parse my movie into tiny little shreds and explain what was wrong with every single one of them. Now, don't get me wrong, Ms. Cherry. I know I'm not a perfect person." Elliot put his hand on his chest and shook his head. "I do know, however, that this is an art form. You can't fight for perfection, or else your creations will never make it out into the world. Life isn't perfect, after all, and isn't that what we're trying to portray here?"

"Certainly." She really had no idea, although she could say that the one scene she'd witnessed them shoot definitely looked like real life. "It's not the same for your films as it is in these big Hollywood movies."

Elliot slapped the table, startling her and those around them. "Yes! Exactly! This is precisely what I'm saying. Ah, I knew I was taking a gamble in agreeing to talk, but I see you are someone who truly understands what it means to be a creative person. I believe Jenny said you do movie reviews?"

Emily concluded that Jenny must be the woman with the headset. "Yes. I've been doing book reviews for a while, but I'm expanding into movies." She hoped that bit of honesty wouldn't make him change his mind about her.

"And you've never worked for the paper before?" His grey eyes caught the sunlight as he studied her.

"Not unless you count the high school paper," she joked.

"Oh, it counts," he assured her with a hint of a curl to his lip that she could only assume was his version of a smile. "But it counts in a much different way than working for a bigtime rag. You see, I firmly believe that our creative experiences when we're young have a huge impact on us as we get older. You may not even have a blog right now if it hadn't been for that stint on the high school paper."

Emily had never imagined that writing about the horrible slop that Mrs. Trundle served up in the cafeteria would truly affect the rest of her life, but she could see his point. "Perhaps not."

"At least it's kept you from being the miserable little creature that Walter Powell is. I have a theory about him, you know." He tapped one finger against the table.

"What's that?" Emily leaned forward, both intrigued by his supposed theory and by the fact that he was speaking of Walter in the present tense. If he knew the critic had been killed, he was doing a good job of covering it up.

"Walter was fired from the *Little Oakley Observer*. That part isn't a theory; it's fact. I discovered from a mutual acquaintance that he was fired for a lack of professionalism. I don't know exactly what was meant by that, but I do know that I agree with it. Anyway, my theory is that he knew he had to create a truly sensational online presence to compete with his former employer. He derided my movie not because he thought it was actually bad, but because he knew an article like that would create far more buzz than talking about the artful way I portrayed the struggle of a young circus performer." Elliot tapped the table once again to drive home his point.

"That's a very interesting observation. It seems to me that you know a lot about the human condition in this line of work." To Emily, what she'd just said sounded like complete drivel.

Elliot, however, ate it up. He gave her another one of those half-smiles. "And you are very astute. You see, it's all about the process…"

Twenty minutes later, Jenny finally dragged Elliot back to his work since all of the cast and crew were waiting on him.

"You be sure to send me a link to your article as soon as it's posted," he said as he got up from the table. He fished in his pockets and produced a ratty business card.

"I'll do that." Emily tucked it inside her notebook, where she'd been obliged to take far more notes from her interview with Elliot than she'd imagined she would.

A short time later, the filming had wrapped up and they were done with Anita as well. "That was fantastic," her friend said as they headed outside. The afternoon sunshine was starting to dissipate, bringing in the chill of autumn. Anita hardly seemed to notice. "I haven't felt that alive in a long time. Don't get me wrong. I know I was just an extra. My online line was, 'Coffee, please,' but that was enough. I'd always wanted to be in a movie, and now I can say I was. Tell me, did I just work for a killer?"

Emily shook her head. "I don't think so. A very passionate man, yes, and one who wasn't very happy about what Walter had to say. He could even be a fantastic liar, making it seem as though he had no idea that his biggest critic was no longer walking this earth. But Elliot Byrne is more concerned with making his movies and getting his message out into the world than on taking revenge. In fact, I didn't even have to bring up Walter. He did that on his own, which also leads me to believe that he didn't have anything to do with it."

"Oh, I'm sorry." Anita pursed her lips. "Here I was reveling in all the glory of my new opportunity, but you didn't get what you needed."

"That's not entirely true," Emily replied with a smile. "He did give me some interesting information. Let's get in the car and get some heat going, and then I'll tell you all about it."

5

"I know, my sweet. I'll get some time with you soon enough. I suppose I get a lot more time at home when I'm reviewing books, but not so much when I'm reviewing movies. Well, all of that has changed for the moment."

Rosemary blinked her big gold eyes and gave Emily a pitiful look.

"I know." Emily was all dressed to go out, but she stooped to give the cat a few more pets. "It's even worse because I'm going out to spend time with other animals. But I promise you, I don't love any of them as much as I love you. You'll always be my favorite."

With a meow, Rosemary scrunched her eyes shut as Emily scratched her head. She hopped up in the big picture window and watched as her owner backed out of the driveway.

There was much to be done in the investigation of Walter Powell's murder. For the moment, though, Emily had other obligations that she couldn't simply set aside. She headed out to Best Friends Furever.

"Good morning, Emily!" Lily Austin greeted her as soon as she walked in. "I'm glad you're here. I haven't been able to decide which pet should be featured on your blog this week."

"You always have some trouble with that," Emily reminded her with a smile. "I can't say that I blame you, because they all deserve plenty of attention."

"That they do," Lily agreed. "I'll let you pick, though." She led the way into the kennel.

The dogs always made a big racket whenever someone came in, but many of them were also wagging their tails and pressing their noses to the chain link as they tried to get closer to Emily. Some of them had been here for quite some time, and so Emily had gotten to know them when she came in to volunteer. "Hello, darling. Yes, it's nice to see you, too. Aw, look at you! You've put on some weight. I can't see all of your ribs anymore. Good job!"

"Here we are." Lily stopped at the end of the row of cages, where a large Staffordshire mix awaited with a wagging tail. "This is Popcorn."

Emily took in the big dog, who was almost entirely white except for a few patches of a pale tan. She had to laugh out loud at the name. "He certainly looks like a large piece of buttered popcorn! I don't think I could turn him down for the blog at all, considering I'm starting on movie reviews!"

"How delightful!" Lily opened the cage to let Popcorn out into the aisle.

He laid his ears down in eager submission as he rushed toward Emily, pressing his head against her knees as he whipped himself with his own tail.

"You're a complete sweetheart, aren't you?" Emily crooned. "I think my readers will absolutely eat you up!"

Lily laughed. "I have a feeling he won't be here long once word gets out about him. He's too sweet and gregarious. Our other option was this girl right over here. Grace is new this week."

Emily peered into the next cage. Soft brown eyes looked back at her with concern and hope. Grace was a terrier mix with short, wiry hair. It was black almost all over, save for a swirl of white near her nose. Unlike Popcorn, she stayed near the back of her cage. She was far less certain of what was going on here at the shelter.

"Poor dear. I take it she's still adjusting?"

"You know how it is," Lily affirmed. "It takes most of them some time to get used to being here, but I worry about her. She's one of those dogs who just has a lot less self-confidence. She's very nervous. I spend time with her when I can, but that isn't often."

Emily's heart went out to her. "Don't you worry, dear. I'll go get some pictures of Popcorn, and then we'll come back to get some pictures of you as well. I'm sure someone would be more than happy to have a gentle little darling like you."

Lily looked at her with just as much hope as Grace did. "Do you think you have space on your blog for both of them, then?"

"Why not? It's my website after all," Emily said with a laugh, feeling the same kind of confidence that Popcorn did. She had worried so much over what to post and if it was the right thing, but she knew she could never go wrong when it came to shelter pets. "Grace needs whatever help I can give, and so I will."

About an hour later, when Emily had finally pulled herself away from all of those darling faces at the shelter, she drove over to the market. She hadn't made a list, and she wished immediately that she had. It was never a good idea to go into the grocery store without a list, and right now seemed even worse. She knew she wanted something specific, but she didn't quite know what.

"You're looking a little lost," a voice commented as she roved into the next aisle.

Emily looked up. Toby had green hair when she'd first met him. He'd changed it to orange, and she thought it might even have been blue at some point, but right now it was a bright purple. It went with all the tattoos on his arms. It all made him look like he might be some sort of punk, but Emily knew that he was one of the nicest people she'd ever met. "Hello, Toby. I suppose I am. You see, I'm planning to have a movie night in with my family."

"Oh, I see. I heard that the cinema was shut down right now after that horrible incident. A movie night at home is probably a very good idea." He reached out and rearranged a can of beans on the shelf, carefully making sure that the label faced forward. "I always liked nachos for a movie snack."

Emily followed him into the next aisle. "Yes, I'm afraid a night at home is the only way to go for me right now. You see, I'm adding movie reviews to my blog. I may not be able to go to the cinema right now, but I figure there are plenty of movies that I can catch up on. What do you like to put on your nachos?"

Toby put a big bag of corn chips into her cart. "You can do just about anything, really. I like black olives, salsa, and of course tons of cheese. My buddies and I sometimes do a big pan and top them with pulled pork or buffalo chicken."

"That doesn't sound like anything that's good for my hips, but certainly good," she said with a smile.

"Oh, definitely. I like guacamole, too." He held up a container of it and then added it to the cart when she nodded. "So you're doing movie reviews now?"

"That's the idea. I've only just started, though." Emily had typed up a rough draft of the action film she'd seen on the same day she'd found Walter's body, but she had yet to post it to her site. It just seemed wrong, considering the police were still looking for the killer.

"What about some gourmet popcorn?" Toby suggested. "The stuff from the cinema is always fantastic in its own right, but regular buttered popcorn at home just isn't the same. You can do some great topping for it that really changes it up, like bourbon caramel."

Emily had to smile and shake her head. "You know, Toby, when I first met you, you told me you didn't do much cooking. You were the one asking me about ingredients, but it seems the tables have turned."

He grinned back at her as he added a few more ingredients to her cart. "I guess you can't work around this food all the time without learning how to use it. I would see something interesting or that looked good, and I'd start experimenting with different recipes. I can't do anything particularly amazing, but I do my best."

"It sounds like you're doing far better than me, right now! Although, I had been concentrating on food and recipes for quite a bit there before I changed it up." In some ways, Emily missed her food blogging days. It meant that she always had something delicious waiting on her in the refrigerator. That food had all gone to her hips, of course.

"Well, the band I was playing with broke up," he explained as they rounded the endcap and went into the next aisle.

"I'm sorry to hear that."

"Nah, don't be." He waved his hand dismissively in the air. "We weren't really creating the sound I wanted, anyway. I think I might be better off working on my music alone. I've saved up and bought some great recording equipment. You know, I was actually thinking about starting a podcast. Maybe just talking about music, playing a few songs, and interviewing other local artists."

"That sounds very nice," Emily enthused. "I certainly wish I'd started doing something like my blog a long time ago, so I think you should go for it."

"Oh, how about an ice cream sundae bar?" Toby asked as they moved into the frozen section. "You set up a few kinds of ice cream with containers of different toppings."

"My granddaughters would absolutely love that!" Emily immediately picked out a large tub of chocolate.

"You just don't want to be like that Walter guy with your movie reviews," Toby commented as he helped her pick out a few different syrups.

She stopped, no longer interested in ice cream. "What do you mean?"

"Well, he did movie reviews, too," Toby began as he contemplated several different containers of sprinkles.

"He never had much nice to say, and all the trolls online would make tons of comments."

"No, I definitely don't want that sort of attention." She'd already decided even before Walter had been killed that she didn't want to be like him. Now she knew for sure that she didn't.

"I mean, the guy made it work," Toby continued as they shopped for fruits and nuts to add to the selection of toppings. "He would dive in and just tear them apart for insulting his work. That was the whole reason I followed him, actually. It wasn't really about the reviews at all but how he was just so good at finding a way to insult someone."

"My goodness!"

"Sorry." Toby's cheeks reddened a bit, an interesting contrast with his purple hair. "I guess that's not what you want to hear."

"No, it's fine," she assured him. It was actually some very good information that very well might help her later. "I just didn't realize. I'd only heard of Walter Powell shortly before his death, and I didn't realize things were that bad on his blog."

"Well, like I said, he made it work for him. I think there were plenty of people who were there for a little bit of humor instead of wondering if they should see the next big flick. Oh, I've got one more suggestion for your movie night. It's over this way."

Emily wasn't feeling quite so enthusiastic about the movie night snacks right now. She had to wonder if this was a new source for suspects. It seemed that Walter Powell had done a fantastic job of making people hate him. The employees and the customers at the cinema, Elliot Byrne, and now anyone who had been angered by his website could all be on the list. How was she going to sort through it all?

"Here we are." They had arrived in the pet care aisle, and Toby took a tiny bag with a picture of a happy gray cat on the front off the shelf. "We just got these treats in last week, and another customer said her cat is nuts for them. I thought Rosemary might like to have a movie night snack as well."

"Aren't you a dear!" Emily took the bag and put it in her cart. "I'll be sure to let her know you picked them out especially for her."

"Only if she likes them!" he laughed. "Have a great movie night!"

"Thank you, Toby. I will."

6

"I'm here to see Jasper Holland, please." Emily lifted her chin and tried to make herself look as confident as possible. She was making quite the habit of demanding to see busy people who probably had no real desire to meet with her. It'd gone well when she'd shown up on the set of Elliot Byrne's latest movie, though. She, Anita, and even Elliot were all going to benefit. That was exactly why she thought she might as well give it another try here at the *Little Oakley Observer*.

The woman at the front desk didn't seem quite so convinced. "Do you have an appointment?" she asked, barely looking up.

"I don't," she admitted, "but I wanted to discuss some article ideas with him if he has a moment." There was no way that the editor of the paper was going to care at all about what she'd written, but getting a job with the paper was the best excuse that she'd been able to think of.

"You and everyone else," the woman mumbled. "What's your name?"

"Emily Cherry."

This got an approving nod from the secretary. "It would look good on a byline. Hold on just a second."

A few minutes later, Emily was escorted through a maze of desks that stretched throughout a long room. People sat at some of them, typing away furiously. Others were on the phone, asking questions and taking notes. Even the desks that weren't occupied were covered in notes, papers, and old editions of the newspaper. At the very back was an office with glass walls. "Emily Cherry to see you," the secretary announced before leaving and closing the door behind her.

"Have a seat." Jasper Holland, or at least, she had to assume he was Jasper Holland since the nameplate on his desk said so, waved vaguely at a chair in front of his desk. The chair had to be at least forty years old, and the brown vinyl upholstery was ripped on two corners, but Emily sat.

"Thank you very much for seeing me," she began, hoping she could find a way to talk about Walter without being too direct.

"I probably shouldn't, to be honest with you." Jasper shuffled through some papers on his desk, sighed, and frowned. He tapped them into a neat stack and set them aside, making no difference in the mess in front of him before he turned to his computer. "I just got back in from an out-of-town trip. The wife wanted to get a vacation in before the weather turned, and of course I obliged. I think everything has fallen apart here while I was gone, though. Anyway, what can I do for you?"

He wasn't even looking at her, but Emily knew that how you carried yourself affected the way you sounded. She sat up straight and folded her hands calmly in front of her. "I've been running my own blog for quite some time now, and I thought the paper might be interested in picking up a few of my articles. Lately I've been specializing in book and movie reviews."

"Oh, boy. Movies. Don't even get me started on movies." He rattled off something on his keyboard, hit the enter key with a loud tap, and then leaned back in his chair.

"Do you not like the cinema, Mr. Holland?"

"Ha! On the contrary, I love the stuff. There's nothing more relaxing than sitting in a dark theater and pretending you're somewhere else for a while. *That's* the kind of vacation that would suit me just fine, instead of heading down to the shore and getting sand in your shoes. No, I suppose my mind has just been a little heavy on the subject ever since I found out that Walter Powell was killed. I suppose you heard about that. It was on our front page, of course."

"Of course." Emily hadn't needed to pick up a copy of *The Observer* to know all the gruesome details, but she kept that information to herself.

"It's a shame that he got himself killed," Jasper continued.

A knock on the door interrupted them, and a young man came in with a stack of mail that he handed to Jasper.

"Thanks, kid. I think. That depends on what's in here. Now, where was I?" he said as they were left alone once again.

"You said something about Walter Powell," Emily reminded him, hoping he wouldn't immediately want to change the subject.

"Oh, yes. Right. Well, I've been thinking about him a lot ever since I found out. And then you add that on top of being on holiday for a week, well, I'm a bit of a mess." Jasper flicked through the stack of mail, frowned again, and stuffed it in a drawer.

"I believe I heard he used to work here?" she ventured.

"He sure did. For quite some time, actually. The man was a terrible mess. My desk looks like a five-star hotel room compared to his. He was constantly late, and he was horrific to the rest of the staff. That was what got him fired, you know. His attitude. Nobody wanted to work

50

with him, and I got so many complaints from people who didn't want to have their desk near his that I hardly knew where to put him anymore."

"That would certainly be a problem," Emily agreed. "I much prefer working from home, myself."

"Right. Yes. You were interested in working for us. Do you have a CV and some samples?"

Fortunately, Emily had come prepared. She handed over a slim folder that contained both her resume and some of her best work. "I've covered quite a few topics in the past, so not all of the articles in there are relevant to what I'm focusing on right now."

Jasper flipped through the papers obligingly. "Well, as far as the movie reviews, I've already got someone on that." He looked up and gestured through the glass wall.

Emily turned to look. A woman sat at a desk far neater than everyone else's. She had trim blonde hair and looked vaguely familiar, but Emily couldn't quite place her. That was what happened when you lived in a small town, though.

"Myla was already doing some smaller bits for us, and she took up the slack when I had to let Walter go. Honestly, for a bit there I thought I'd have to let her go, as well." The editor had set aside her folder. He then picked up another stack of papers on his desk and began sorting through them, tossing several into the recycling bin.

"Do your readers not look to the paper for movie reviews any longer?" With as many people as there were writing online, Emily wouldn't be surprised.

"It isn't that, really. It's that Walter's blog was doing so incredibly well. He made for some very stiff competition, and I was starting to juggle whether or not that space would be better used for more advertisements or a different kind of article. You only have so much real estate in the paper, you know. You have to use it wisely. I can't tell you how much I have to reject every day."

"I'm sure that's true. I guess Walter was quite popular, wasn't he?" So far, Emily hadn't really learned anything she hadn't known before other than the fact that Walter kept his desk messy. This might be a complete waste of time.

Jasper let out a small laugh. "You could put it that way, but I think it had more to do with all the commenters. Someone would jump on there and deride him for his article. Then the guy would actually screenshot it, repost it, and proceed to disparage them so badly even their ancestors would be insulted. That was what really drew people in, I think. I try to run an honest paper here, so I can't use that sort of energy to keep the paper going."

"No, of course not."

"Anyway, I thought I'd have to let Myla go and stop the movie reviews altogether. I suppose now that Walter is gone, I won't have to worry about that. For now. We'll see how it goes." Jasper put her file aside on top of more paper. "I tell you what. Your writing looks like pretty decent stuff. If I had the space, I'd probably ask you to come on as a regular columnist. I don't, but if you have an article you're particularly proud of, you feel free to send it my way."

Emily sensed this short and strange interview as over, and she stood. "Thank you very much for your time, Mr. Holland. I'll be sure to do that."

He shook her hand, and she showed herself out of his office.

The large office area that the rest of the staff used was a maze, and so it was easy enough for Emily to take a slight detour by Myla's desk. Walter's replacement might have some insight on her predecessor, after all. She smiled at the pretty blonde, but she couldn't think of a single thing to say to her. Perhaps she'd used up all of her talents in getting interview with both Elliot Byrne and Jasper Holland.

Myla's desk was unlike those around her in its neatness, but also in its décor. The writer had personalized everything within reach using a bumblebee theme. Her pencil cup had a crocheted cover in yellow and black stripes. Her coffee mug looked like a honeycomb, and her mousepad reminded everyone to 'Bee Happy.' A small calendar showed a monthly display of bees on flowers, and even her paperweight was a giant bee. It was all so bright and pretty, a springlike display amongst all the white and gray that made up the office. Emily thought perhaps her own desk at home could use a sprucing up.

As she headed back outside to her car, she had to wonder if Jasper Holland belonged on her suspect list. He hadn't liked Walter very much, and the writer had certainly caused a lot of trouble for him and for the paper. Jasper had claimed that he'd just gotten back from out of town. That might be a good alibi, but it wasn't one that Emily would easily be able to verify. Then again, why would he bother giving her his alibi when he had no idea she was investigating Walter's murder? It seemed that her foray to the *Little Oakley Observer* had left her with more questions than answers.

7

"Look, Gran! Mum let us wear our pajamas!" Ella announced proudly as she and Lucy came bursting in the door.

Emily came out of the kitchen. "Well, look at that! You certainly are! You're going to be very cozy and comfortable tonight. I've got everything all set up in my guest bedroom for you."

"But I thought we were going to get to watch the movies with you guys!" Lucy protested.

"Darling, it's a movie for grownups. Gran rented a special movie just for the two of you," Phoebe explained to her girls.

"I think you're really going to like it," Emily added. She and Phoebe had gotten together on the movie, so she knew the girls hadn't seen it yet.

Lucy folded her arms over her chest, nearly dropping the blanket she'd brought in. "But I'm eight! I shouldn't have to watch baby movies like Ella!"

"I'm not a baby!" Ella protested.

"All right, girls. That's enough." Matthew stepped inside, carrying the rest of the girls' things, including all the stuffed animals and pillows they'd insisted on bringing along. "Gran has gone to the trouble to make sure the two of you can have a nice evening. You owe her a little bit of appreciation and respect, and that doesn't include fussing at each other."

"All right," Lucy conceded begrudgingly.

Emily very much wanted the two of them to have a good night. "If you're very good, I've got a special dessert ready to go for you."

"You do?" Lucy's eyes went wide, and she forgot all about having to watch the kids' movie. "What is it?"

"It's a surprise," Emily reminded her with a smile. "You'll have to make sure you eat some dinner and get along nicely with your sister, and then you'll get to find out!"

"Come on, Ella." Lucy put her arm around her sister's shoulders and guided her down the hallway. "I'll let you cuddle with Stardust for the first half of the movie."

Phoebe raised her brows. "That must be some phenomenal dessert if Lucy is actually giving up her unicorn for any amount of time."

Nathan and Genevieve arrived next, dressed to the nines as they always were.

"You're not going to be comfortable in that," Emily protested as she tugged teasingly on Nathan's suit jacket. "You should've gone home and changed after work."

"Don't be silly, Mother. I'm always comfortable in a suit." He bent to kiss her cheek.

"And you look good in it, too," Genevieve agreed. "Emily, was that information about Elliot Byrne helpful to you?"

"Oh, very," she confirmed as she pulled the hot tray of nachos out of the oven. "I found him on his set and got to speak with him for quite some time."

"You did?" The gorgeous and influential Genevieve, who probably wouldn't be startled by meeting even the most glamorous celebrity, leaned forward with her eyes wide. "He actually let you onto the set? And you got to talk with him?"

Emily tried not to laugh, but it was hard considering she'd almost never seen her daughter-in-law behave like this. "Oh, yes. He was quite busy with his work, and he was very involved with it, but he was also very chatty. I'll be doing a piece entirely about him soon." Once all of this with Walter cleared up, anyway.

"I just can't believe it," Genevieve mumbled, tossing back her blonde hair. "I thought he was one of those artsy types who had to work in an environment entirely of his own making."

"Then you might want to see where's he's shooting next and go down there. Anita even got to be an extra."

Genevieve slapped the counter, her heavily lined eyes wide than ever. "What?"

"Who's talking about me?" Anita asked as she threaded her way into the kitchen. "I brought the wine, so no worries."

"You've got to tell me all about your time with Elliot Byrne!" Genevieve demanded.

Anita chuckled, but she also tipped back her head a little. She was feeling special, and Emily couldn't blame her. "I suppose I have a minute."

"Well, they're going to be busy most of the night," Nathan commented as he reached over to swipe a nacho. "Genny said you were interested in movies for your blog. I don't suppose you know anything about this Walter Powell and his death?"

She ignored the serious look her son gave her. He was her oldest child and her only son, and ever since Sebastian had passed away, he'd seemed to think he needed to take care of her. Emily could appreciate it for what it was, but she also knew she could take care of herself just fine. "I did hear about that," she replied simply.

"I hope you're staying out of trouble," he pressed.

Emily gave that one a thought for a moment. She'd gone and done some interesting interviews, and she'd learned some interesting things, but she couldn't say she'd gotten herself in any kind of trouble. "I am. Now stay out of the nachos until we get started. I don't want you to eat them all and not leave any for the rest of us."

Mavis showed up last, dressed comfortably in joggers and a sweatshirt and lugging a cat carrier. "I'm sorry I'm late. Gus was nowhere to be found when I got home from work. I think he's upset with me for being gone so much."

"Then he and Rosemary will have a lot to talk about," Emily replied, looking around under the dining table where she'd last seen her cat. "I've been gone from the house far more than usual, and she's not happy about it. The last time I tried to leave the house, she practically stood in front of the door and demanded that I stay home!"

When Mavis opened the door to Gus's carrier, Rosemary suddenly appeared. She and the pale cat sniffed each other in greeting before trotting off to play in the box of cat toys Emily had assembled in the corner of the living room.

Soon enough, everyone was settled in. Lucy and Ella were tucked into the big bed in the guest bedroom, surrounded by an infinite number of blankets, pillows, and plushies. They were told they were allowed to eat in bed for a change, and that someone would get them when it was time for dessert. Nathan took off his suit jacket and loosened his tie before settling in on the couch next to Genevieve in her designer blouse and slacks. Emily and Anita chose the loveseat, and Mavis settled into an armchair. The cats soon stopped playing and settled in with their respective owners.

"I'm not surprised that you chose a mystery," Mavis said as the opening credits began. "Those seem to be your favorite things lately."

"I can't deny that," Emily agreed. "I thought it might be a nice change of pace from the last couple of movies I've seen anyway."

Emily took a deep breath and relaxed. She truly did love going to the cinema. As Jasper Holland had stated, sitting in that big dark theater and pretending you were somewhere else for a while could be a nice vacation. Being at home could be just as satisfying, however. Leaning over, Emily picked up the notepad she's set on the end table for just this purpose. She would review the movie itself, regardless of its age, but there was no reason she couldn't also do a post simply on the merits of a movie night in. There was the fact that the food cost far less, for one thing. She couldn't deny the benefits of being able to pause the film, which they would undoubtedly need to do at some point. Emily was also incredibly comfortable on her own furniture.

"Are you working?" Anita whispered. In the light from the television, her eyes glittered.

"Of course," Emily replied.

With a nod and a smile, Anita returned her attention to the movie.

Emily would do the same shortly, but she first had to jot down a quick note about how having Rosemary on her lap was perhaps the biggest benefit of all when it came to watching at home.

She stroked her hands through Rosemary's thick fur, feeling the cat's purrs dissipate as she fell asleep. Emily thought she could just about fall asleep herself, even as they mystery slowly unfolded on the screen before her. It was obvious to her who the villains were. They *looked* evil as well as acting it. There was no doubt in her mind they were the killers.

She sat up a little straighter during the next scene. The villains knew the hero was on their tail, and so they'd asked him to go on a hunting trip Emily felt her muscles tense as all of her fears flooded into her, ones that she'd set aside for a long time because she knew they were just a result of her overactive mind. But the more she watched, the less she could handle.

"Excuse me." Setting a surprised Rosemary aside, Emily headed off to her bedroom.

Anita's soft knock came on the door a minute later. "I don't mean to bother you if it's just that the nachos aren't sitting right," she said as she peeked around the door, "but I had a feeling that wasn't it."

"Shut the door." Emily grabbed a tissue from the nightstand and pressed it to her cheeks. "I'm afraid I've made a very poor choice of movie."

"Is that why you're upset?" Anita sat carefully on the end of the bed next to her. "You're worried that everyone isn't having a good time."

"It's not that." Emily took a breath, trying to figure out how she could get all of this into words. "It's just that scene we were watching. They took Malcolm out into the woods on a supposed hunting trip. They were never going to let him live through it, of course. Now, it's a movie and we all know it has to have a happy ending, so Malcolm is going to be just fine. I just can't help thinking that something very similar may have happened to my Sebastian."

Anita put her hand on Emily's knee. "You've mentioned something along those lines before."

"Yes, and I decided I was just trying too hard to find some sort of reason behind his loss. People die in accidents every day, and there's no reason behind it. And of course I miss him terribly, so it's not as though I can ever just truly accept that he's gone. But Anita, the more I think on it, the more I have to wonder." She dabbed at her face once again, hoping that she wasn't puffing up too much. Then everyone would know she was upset.

Anita sat with her in silence for a while. "Have you talked to the kids about it?" she asked.

"No, and I won't," Emily affirmed. "Not unless I truly have some sort of evidence. I wouldn't want to worry them for nothing if it turns out I'm wrong. I'm sure they wouldn't like to think their father met such a fate. Besides, you know Nathan. He'll probably lock me in my room if he thinks I'm going to go after another murderer."

They both had to laugh a little at that one.

"Do you want to do something about it?" Anita brushed Emily's hair off the back of her neck.

Oh, she was so lucky to have such a sweet friend! Anita was confident and sassy. She wouldn't hesitate to put anyone in their place if she thought they needed it, and she didn't mind making a scene. She could also be incredibly gentle and understanding.

"I think I do," Emily admitted, "eventually. Maybe not right at this moment, but it does feel a little bit better just to have it off my chest for now."

"That's what I'm here for. I have no doubt that Alyssa would be happy to help when she gets back in town, as well. But whatever you want to do, I'm here for you." Anita patted her on the shoulder with finality, as though there was no way that anyone could contest her words.

Emily certainly wasn't going to. "Thank you. I suppose I should clean myself up and get back out there before anyone starts to wonder what happened to us."

When they stepped into the hall a few minutes later, they were greeted by Lucy and Ella as they came out of the guest room. "Is it time for dessert yet?" Ella asked sweetly.

Emily reached out and took her hand, reveling in how warm and sweet it was. "I think we can make that happen. Let's go."

8

"That really was a wonderful time," Mavis said, stretching and yawning. Gus, who had been almost permanently glued to her lap for the evening, rolled his head to the side and stretched his long white legs in agreement.

"I think so, too. We'll have to do it again sometime." Emily looked down at the notes she'd written. There was enough there to put together the post about having movie night at home, but she wouldn't be writing about the movie itself. She'd managed to catch most of it despite her little trip down the hallway, but she'd be hard pressed to know what to say about it. That it made her think of her deceased husband? That she might have a much bigger and more important mystery to solve than the one in the movie? No, she would just forget about it for now.

"You seem distracted," Mavis noted. She turned a little so that she leaned on the arm of the chair and studied her mother. "In fact, you've been that way for a good part of the night. What's wrong?"

"Oh, nothing." Emily knew that what she'd said to Anita was the right thing. There was no point in unsettling her children with the idea that what had happened to their father wasn't a simple accident. She didn't like to keep secrets from them, and she liked to think they had a mature, adult relationship, but still.

Mavis tipped her head to one side. "You've got something to do with Walter Powell's death, don't you?"

Slowly, Emily's eyes slid up from the notebook to meet her youngest daughter's. Well, that wasn't so much of a secret, not really. "Why would you say a thing like that?" she asked innocently.

The grin that took over Mavis's face rivaled that of her cat. "Well, let's see. First of all, there's the fact that you're blogging about movies. I know that whatever topic you get interested in, it becomes your current obsession."

"There are plenty of people who write about the movies," Emily reminded her.

"Very true," Mavis agreed, "but there's one less in the world right now. You haven't said a thing about it, which makes me think you must be trying to make sure Nathan doesn't find out. Not that I blame you," she added quickly.

"Then," Mavis continued, drawing her feet up onto the cushion and slightly dislodging Gus, "there's the fact that you've hardly been home all week. I'm sure you could argue that it's because you've been going to the movies and the market, but I hardly think you'd go to the cinema every day."

Propping her chin on her hand, Emily smiled. "You know, I don't think I'm the only sleuth in the room."

"So who's your current suspect?" Mavis rubbed her hands together eagerly, earning herself a disgruntled look from Gus.

Rosemary had quickly parked herself right back on Emily's lap when she'd emerged from the bedroom midway through the movie, and then she'd done it again once Emily was done saying goodbye to everyone when they'd turned the lights on. The sweet little thing stretched her paws out on Emily's leg and snuggled her head in, showing her appreciation.

"That's a mighty long list," Emily admitted. "I've managed to eliminate a few people from it, but not enough. I can't even check in with Alyssa, because she's still out of town for a few more days. I'm afraid she's going to have an interesting case on her hands if they put it on her desk for her to tackle when she returns."

"What have you done so far?" Mavis buried her fingers in the thick white fur of Gus's belly.

Emily leaned back in her chair. She'd kept most of this investigation to herself, with Anita being the only other person she'd really involved. She loved her children, though, and it was nice to let them in on what she had going on. Emily told her of finding Walter at the cinema and the theories she and the employees had gone over while they waited for police. Everyone knew that she'd gone to visit the set of Elliot Byrne's latest film, but she hadn't revealed that it was because she'd suspected him. Then, of course, there was her little interview at the paper. Mavis listened to it all raptly. She was a grown woman now, with a career and her own apartment, but she still reminded Emily so much of the little girl who used to get more and more awake as she listened to her bedtime stories instead of falling asleep.

"So, what's next?" Mavis sat up straighter in her chair when Emily was done. She wrapped an arm around the sleepy Gus to keep him from falling off her lap. "Is there anything I can help with?"

"It's funny, you know. Nathan is always wanting me to stay out of these things because he thinks he's protecting me. I, on the other hand, worry about involving you children too much because I want to protect you," Emily noted.

A slow smile spread over Mavis's face as she thought about what might make her big brother angry. "Then I promise not to tell Nathan," she said with a quirk of one eyebrow.

It was late. Emily had been through a lot that day, what with cleaning the house, cooking enough food to have everyone over, and then of course the emotional exhaustion her movie selection had caused her. By all means, she ought to be dragging her poor old body to bed. Her mind, however, was suddenly whirring again. "You know, I've been trying to decide that. I don't have anyone else specific that I can track down and talk to. Elliot Byrne and Jasper Holland were my best suspects, since I knew he'd worked with them directly. Everyone, however, seems to know what a stir Walter always caused online. I suppose that means it's time to finally look him up."

"I'll get your laptop," Mavis volunteered. "Is it on your desk?"

"As always." Emily picked up her own sleepy cat and deposited her on the couch next to Gus. "I'm sorry, you two. I know you're having a wonderful time, but you'll have to excuse us while we get some things taken care of."

Mavis returned a moment later, carrying the laptop like a trophy and walking quickly through the house in her stocking feet. She swiped a handful of bourbon caramel popcorn and parked herself on the loveseat next to her mother. "What was this guy's name again?"

Emily was more than happy to let her do the searching. Mavis, after all, worked for a tech company and knew plenty about computers. Emily got along well enough with her computer for what she needed, but Mavis was still the expert. "Walter Powell. It should be a movie blog. I assume that he probably wrote under his own name, since everyone seemed to know who he was."

"Easy enough," Mavis announced as she clicked onto a page. "He's right here, front and center. Looks like he had plenty of traffic, so he was easy to find. It hasn't been updated since his death, of course."

"Is he really as terrible as everyone says?" Emily leaned over to get a better look, skimming through the post titles. Most of them were obviously movie reviews, but there was several with headlines like 'This Guy Thinks He Knows Something' and 'Get a Load of This.'

"Let's find out." Mavis clicked on a movie review first and read aloud. "If you're thinking about heading to the cinema to see *Trees of the Light,* then don't waste your money. With the ever-rising cost of tickets, plus the fact that one almost has to take out a loan to pay for concessions, films these days need to be true hits. There's no reason for them not to be, considering all the resources that are at the hands of even the lowest of filmmakers. Apparently, those who made *Trees of Light* don't realize that. Even for a low-budget film, it doesn't come close to holding up the expectations set forth in the trailers. The acting was stiff, and the dialog was just as wooden as the supposed trees in the title. I could've made the same movie in my backyard with nothing more than a cell phone and a cardboard cutout of my favorite celebrity."

"Wow. Even if it was that bad, he didn't even try to find something nice to say about it," Emily mused.

Mavis nodded as she scrolled down. "It served him well, though. He got tons of comments, so you know there were even more views than that. Walter replied to most of them, too."

Emily scanned through the remarks. "And this is exactly my problem. If there were so many people who despised him, then how am I to pick one out of the crowd to pursue?"

"I imagine the police are having the same issue," Mavis added. She moved to another post.

In this one, Walter wasn't lambasting a movie. He had taken a screenshot of a comment, enlarged it, and ranted against the poster. "This is what Toby down at the market was telling me about."

"The comment must have really stood out for him." Mavis scrolled past the screenshot and read aloud once again. "I see you have once again decided to visit my blog. I can't for the life of me figure out why you would do such a thing, since you obviously hate it. If you like to torture yourself, though, then that's your problem. Now, should we start with your grammar, punctuation, or the fact that you're completely wrong?"

It went on from there, but Emily had heard enough. "It's hard for me to understand how anyone can consider this entertainment. They're both being so mean to each other, and there's no reason for it."

"Well, whoever this is, they really must have had it out for Walter. This same screen handle is one that Walter has turned around and attacked multiple times. That's kind of funny."

"What's that?"

Mavis was looking through the posts and comments again. "Oh, everyone has a different username, and sometimes people choose funny ones. There are a lot of movie themed ones on here, which makes sense. There's DrNope, ScarlettTheHare, and LarryofArabia. The one that he seems to have had the biggest battle with is PlanetoftheApiaries."

"I don't suppose there's any way of finding out who they are in real life, is there?" Emily asked. Looking up Walter's blog would've been easy enough, but the rest of it would be far beyond her expertise.

"Not unless they've done something to give themselves away elsewhere. It looks like this blog platform allows people to create whatever user information they'd like, and there's nothing that verifies their identity or ties them back to a real name. That doesn't mean they haven't used the same handle elsewhere, though. You give me some time, and I can see if I can figure it out," Mavis offered.

It was a safe enough thing for her to do, and so Emily nodded. "All right. You let me know as soon as you find out, though."

"Of course." Mavis exited the browser and shut down the computer. "For now, though, I think it's all time we went to bed. Come on, Gus. You can come get more snuggles with Rosemary another time."

The two cats had curled up in a swirl of contrasting cat fur on the sofa. Mavis picked up a reluctant Gus, put him in his carrier, and headed home.

Emily moved slowly through the room, picking up the last few dishes and putting away the leftovers, which she'd refused to let Mavis help her with. Her youngest daughter had already helped her enough. The sundae bar had left a sticky mess on the kitchen counter, but it made Emily smile to remember just how much her granddaughters had loved it.

Getting a hot wet rag, Emily thought about what she'd seen on Walter's blog. Both he and this PlanetoftheApiaries person had been very wrong to speak to each other that way. They probably thought they could hide behind their computers and say whatever they wanted. Maybe they could, if the killer proved to be someone that Walter dealt with in real life. Even so, she knew she would never let her own blog take on the same tone that his had. She loved her readers, and as far as she could tell they loved her. Emily wanted to keep it that way.

9

Emily's heart thumped in her chest as she parked and walked across the street. The cinema had reopened. It was only right that it'd stayed closed for a time after what had happened there, but it couldn't remain so forever. She squared her shoulders and forced her footsteps to be more determined as she approached. Emily hadn't really wanted to go back, not after what she'd seen. But how would she add movie reviews to her blog if she never went to see a movie? And could she really just stay away forever? No. She'd told herself quite some time ago that she wanted to be braver, bolder. There was no time like the present.

Whispers of the Future would be starting in about fifteen minutes, which meant the crowd was already shuffling in. They would get here early to claim their concessions and their seats, and then they would gossip while the trailers played, wondering exactly where the man had been killed. It was probably some sort of excitement for them, Emily thought, a peek of real life that they normally only got through the fictional world that they'd come here to see this afternoon. For them, it would be something to talk about with their friends after dinner. Emily wasn't sure that she wanted to talk about it at all.

Though she hardly needed any food, Emily joined the queue for snacks. She deserved a little treat just for being courageous enough to walk through these doors. She read the menu, but her mind refused to understand the words. It only wanted to concentrate on Walter.

Mavis hadn't yet gotten anywhere on their search for the internet troll who had stalked Walter's website so regularly. She'd had a lot going on at work that morning, so there had been precious little time for her to get around to it. She would, she promised. Emily had assured her that she wasn't disappointed, only curious. It might very well be just as much of a dead end as everything else. Still, she'd made herself a note to ask Alyssa if Walter had ever asked for a protective order against someone. It was a long shot, but it could be a worthwhile lead.

"No, I'm sorry. I wanted a large popcorn, please," the woman in front of Emily said, pushing the small popcorn she'd just been handed back across the counter. "That's what I get every time, after all."

The young man behind the counter was one that Emily didn't know. His cheeks flushed a violent shade of red as he mumbled an apology and took the popcorn.

Poor thing. Emily knew it wasn't easy for young folks to learn how to navigate their jobs successfully. The woman could've been nicer about it, she thought. Well, Emily would do what she could to make up for it. She would be sure to find a way to compliment him.

When the woman in front of her had received the snack she wanted and turned to go to her theater, Emily noticed the fuzzy bumblebee earrings dangling from her ears beneath her curtain of blonde hair. She'd certainly been seeing a lot of bees lately, she thought. Then she paused as she realized that she'd seen this woman before. Twice, in fact. She was the same blonde that Mason and Zoe had pointed out as one of their regulars, and she was also the woman who worked at *The Little Oakley Observer* as Walter's replacement. Well, that made a lot of sense. She would need to be a regular here at the cinema if she were going to write movie reviews.

"Can I help you?" the young man behind the counter asked nervously.

"Yes, I'd like a popcorn and a soda, please." She turned her head to see Myla walking off to the left toward the theater where her movie would be shown. Perhaps she would be a good person to interview for her blog, since her position at the paper meant she was the most official movie critic in town. With her other planned posts about movie night at home and Elliot Byrne, a little bit of time with Myla could help her build up quite the list in the movie category on her blog.

"There you are." The clerk eyed her nervously.

"Thank you very much. You were very quick about that. I'll be sure to tell your manager," Emily promised with a smile. She would likely stop and talk to Mason while she was here. After she'd sat in his office with him and Zoe while waiting for the police, she felt they were all quite close. At the moment, he was in his office with the door open, going over some paperwork. The movie was about to start, so she'd catch him later.

In the theater, Emily nestled into her seat. She knew a notepad wouldn't help her much in here, and she wasn't going to be obnoxious enough to use her cell phone, so any thoughts she had about the movie would just have to stick around long enough for her to jot them down later. And when she did, she promised herself, she would sit right in the middle of the lobby where everyone could see her instead of trying to find a private spot.

The trailers finished and the opening scene began. Emily knew she should focus on the movie. That was why she was here. But she couldn't help but look around at the other viewers around her. A couple sat with their arms around each other. A man sat by himself, nursing a giant soda. A row of teenagers giggled with each other excitedly. Even Myla was there, unmistakable with those bee earrings that made fuzzy little silhouettes against the silver screen. Walter had been one of them, once. He'd come in and sat down, not having any idea that the movie would be the last one he saw. It was terribly sad, even if he hadn't been a very kind man.

Emily's eyes landed on those earrings once again, and the pieces of the puzzle began to click into place. Walter had worked for the paper. Myla might lose her job. Someone had been trolling Walter online, far more than anyone else. A swirling ball of nerves and nausea formed in her stomach. What was she to do? She couldn't call the police department. Alyssa wasn't there and nobody else would believe the ramblings of an old woman.

The movie went on without Emily paying a lick of attention, trying only to think of what she might do. She still hadn't come to a conclusion when Myla got up halfway through the film and stepped into the aisle. As casually as she could, Emily slipped past the people sitting next to her and followed.

"Excuse me," she said, catching up as they stepped into the long hall that all the theaters opened up into.

Myla paused, her empty popcorn in her hand. She looked mildly irritated. "Yes?"

"You're Myla Gordon, aren't you?" Emily smiled at her and did her best to look completely enchanted. "You write for *The Observer?*"

"I do," Myla admitted, now smiling. "What can I do for you?"

"Well, I'm a bit of a writer myself, and I was just wondering if you would have some time to do a little interview for me. I'd like to feature you on my blog. Not today, of course. We could schedule it for some other time this week." Emily thought she would be a good subject if she happened to be innocent, but she'd also have time to contact Alyssa and get all of her ducks in a row.

"Oh. No. I'm afraid I don't do things like that." Myla turned and continued toward the concession counter.

"It really would mean a lot to me," Emily insisted. She had to find some way of speaking to her to tease out the truth. "I don't want to inconvenience you at all, but it might be rather fun."

"No. I said no." Myla took several more steps toward the main part of the lobby.

"Please." Emily wanted to reach out and grab her sleeve, but she yanked her hand back as Myla turned.

"Why on earth would you want to interview someone who writes the tiniest column at the paper?" Myla demanded. "You're just as terrible as that awful clerk who doesn't know how to fetch the right size of popcorn."

Emily's mouth tightened. "I see. It turns out you know how to say awful, scathing things whether you're on the computer or speaking to someone in real life."

"What do you mean?" Myla demanded.

There was nothing she could do to hold it back now. It was all right there in front of her, and Emily couldn't believe she hadn't seen it before. "You killed Walter Powell."

The woman's eyes went wide, and she nearly dropped her popcorn bag. "What makes you think you can make such wild accusations?"

"Because I've got all the proof I need to know it's the truth," Emily insisted. "It would take someone very mean and very desperate to do such a thing. You don't look like it on the outside, but I'm quite certain you know how to insult something with hardly any thought, Myla. Or should I say, PlanetoftheApiaries!"

Though it wouldn't have seemed possible, Myla's blue eyes went even wider. Her jaw tightened, and her lips moved around her clenched teeth as she tried to figure out what to say. Unable to find anything quite right, she launched herself at Emily. Her hands went straight for Emily's throat.

Stepping backward, Emily wasn't quick enough to dodge out of the way. She slammed into one of the big framed movie posters on the wall. The edge of it dug into her back. Fear trickled down Emily's spine. Nathan had warned her that this could be dangerous. She'd hate to think he might be right.

The movie poster swung dangerously as Emily slid to the floor, making a horrid scraping sound against the wall. "Yes, I killed him," Myla growled. "I did what I had to do, and I won't hesitate to do it again."

Emily fought to get her fingers between Myla's hands and her own neck. She wished that she was stronger, but this woman was far younger than she was. "You can't do this. You don't have the movie to cover your tracks this time."

"I don't need it. You're old. Maybe you got too excited and keeled over from a heart attack!"

Myla's enraged face was all Emily could see. Her heart did indeed pound in her chest as she thought about her children, her friends, and her dear Rosemary. This woman didn't understand just what she was trying to do, how many people it would affect. Was it the same for Walter? Was someone grieving him somewhere?

"Get back!" a deep voice thundered. Myla's face quickly disappeared, leaving Emily to stare only at the ceiling. "Xavier, call the police! And an ambulance!"

Emily blinked up to see that Mason was standing over her, holding the snarling Myla by the back of her shirt. "Don't listen to that crazy old bat! She's insane!"

A moment later, Zoe's face appeared over Emily's. She gently touched her cheek as her eyes narrowed with concern. "Emily? The ambulance is on its way. Are you all right?"

The wind had been knocked out of her when she'd fallen to the floor, and there would surely be a bruise across her back where she'd hit the poster frame. But Walter's killer was about to get the justice she deserved. "Tell your management I'd like to lodge a complaint about another patron."

10

"You really don't have to go to any trouble," Alyssa Bradley insisted as she nervously watched Emily bring out the tea service. "I came by to talk, and I was already worried that was going to be too much for you."

"It's no trouble at all," Emily insisted as she poured a cup of tea for her guest. "The doctor said getting up and moving around was good for me. It'll help keep the aches and pains away, and I need to get more exercise, anyway. I have a few bumps and bruises, but it's all recoverable."

"It might've been much worse if Myla had figured out earlier what you were really about and had decided to plot her revenge against you the way she did Walter," Alyssa commented with a pointed look.

Emily gave her one right back as she straightened. "Are you suggesting that I should've left it all for the police?"

Alyssa let out a breathy laugh. "No, I don't suppose I can say that at all, can I? It just worried me when I came back and found out what had happened. I do hope you're truly all right."

Rosemary marched into the room with her tail in the air. She lifted her nose to sniff, and when she found that there wasn't any particularly interesting food on the tea tray, she proceeded to wind herself several times around Alyssa's ankles.

Easing herself down onto the sofa, Emily smiled at her sweet pet. "I am, and I'll be more all right if you can tell me all of the details that I missed. I know there must be something, even if I did collar the right person."

Alyssa gave Rosemary an obligatory scratch behind the ears before she took a sip of tea. "These things are rarely ever simple, but I'd say you had most of it down pat. Myla had been wanting to get a job at the paper for a long time. She'd been submitting articles while also trying to set herself up as a freelance writer. Things weren't really panning out for her, not until Walter got himself fired, anyway."

"That's a shame, you know," Emily commented quietly. "I don't know what makes people behave the way they do, sometimes. He might've gone on to have a long, steady career at *The Observer* otherwise."

"Yes, I think so. But his personality just wasn't suited for it, I guess you could say. Myla was thrilled with the new position she was suddenly offered after trying so hard for so long, but it was threatened almost immediately. Walter had enough of a reputation built up before he was fired, and it carried over when he launched his own website. Yes, you really are a darling, aren't you?" This last was directed at Rosemary, who was rubbing her wiry whiskers against Alyssa's leg.

"She knows good people when she sees them," Emily noted.

"Then perhaps you should take her out with you when you start investigating," Alyssa replied with laughter in her bright eyes. "She'd probably tell you right away if someone had criminal tendencies."

Emily stirred some honey into her tea. "Don't think I haven't thought about it! I'm not sure Rosemary would appreciate it, though. She's rather a homebody. Do continue, though."

"Ah, yes." Alyssa took another sip of tea and refocused herself on her main purpose of coming here. "Myla needed Walter's blog to bomb in order to keep her job secure. She started making terrible comments, insulting him for his reviews. It seems she thought that if he left enough negative comments, it would deter his readers and drive down his traffic."

"Instead, it only made him more popular," Emily concluded, twisting up her mouth as she thought about that. "He made the whole thing into a sport, which had the added benefit of creating more material for his website. People like to see a fight, don't they?"

"It would seem so," Alyssa agreed. "We witness it even in real life. If the police are called, say, because two men are having a brawl outside a pub, you can just about guarantee there will be a crowd of people standing there to watch it. Most of them will be getting it on video, too. None of them are actually doing anything about it, though."

"A shame," Emily tsked.

Alyssa sighed. "At any rate, Myla realized that everything she was doing to bring Walter down was only helping him. She grew desperate. The vast amount of time she spent at the cinema meant that she had a distinct advantage when it came to Walter. She knew his schedule and what movies he'd been to. She also knew the movies themselves rather well, often seeing the same film two or three times in order to write the most detailed reviews that she could."

"That was how she knew exactly when she could pull the trigger without causing mass hysteria at the cinema," Emily supplied. "I must admit that it bothers me quite a lot to know I heard the gunshot and didn't do anything about it."

"You couldn't have known," Alyssa reminded her gently. "And even if you did, what could you have done about it? Myla was armed and dangerous."

"Dangerous, all right," Emily agreed, "even without a gun."

"Yes, it would seem. Tell me, how did you find out that it was Myla? There had to be something that brought you around to that conclusion."

"Oh, yes. There was, although I'm ashamed that I hadn't put it all together earlier. You see, there were so many people who had a cause to dislike Walter that I was starting to think I'd never be able to sort through enough of them and actually find the killer. Knowing that Myla was in danger of losing her job if Walter's blog succeeded should've been enough to lead me in that direction, but it was actually the décor on her desk?"

Alyssa squinted. "Her desk?"

"Yes, indeed." Emily could still see it all in her mind, clear as day. "It was absolutely covered in cute little bees. It was bright and pretty compared to the rest of the dreary newspaper office, and I'm ashamed to admit the first thing it made me think was that I should spruce up my own desk. But then there were the little bumblebee earrings she wore at the cinema."

"A natural carryover, if she liked them that much," Alyssa said.

"Yes, and nothing to think of at all. The real clue was the screen name of the person Walter had loathed the most, teased the most. PlanetoftheApiaries. It was a funny play on the old movies, but it also gave away quite a bit of information. Whoever used that name obviously liked the cinema, and they obviously liked bees, since an apiary is where bees are kept. Myla fit both of those descriptions to a tee."

"My goodness." Alyssa shook her head and clucked her tongue. "That really is quite simple once you have all the information, isn't it?"

"Yes, I think so. And then, as I told you, Mavis was able to track down the screen name and tie it to Myla Gordon. That was after I'd already had my confrontation with her, so it was too late in that regard. Still, it was nice to have the confirmation. Don't ask me what Mavis did to find out, though. The girls knows more about computers than I ever will."

Alyssa set her cup down on the tray. She leaned forward, bracing her elbows on her knees, and studied Emily closely. "Does this mean you'll stop doing movie reviews?"

That was something Emily had thought long and hard about over the last few days. "You know, I've often changed the topic of my blog at the drop of a hat. I never felt badly about it, even when my son Nathan warned me that I might lose readers. It's mine, after all, and I think I should make it just what I want it to be. It took me a while to figure out exactly what that is, but I'm coming closer."

"And that is?" Alyssa looked down as Rosemary came back for another round of attention, reaching up to rub her cheeks against one of the detective's dangling hands Giving up, Alyssa scooped her into her lap.

"I very much like doing book reviews, and I don't want to give that up," Emily began. "The other ideas I had were nice, but they weren't really *me*. The books are, as I've always loved them. I still love sharing them with the world. I think the movies are a natural overflow of that, since so many people like to compare the book and the movie that is made from it. It's all about the story, whichever way you look at it."

Rosemary's purr thundered through the room as she kneaded her front paws against Alyssa's leg.

"That's very true." Alyssa was quiet for a while. She took in a breath as though she was about to speak, but then she let it out without saying anything.

"Go on with it," Emily encouraged, "otherwise I'll wonder what it was, and I won't be able to sleep at night. You wouldn't want to keep an old woman from getting her rest."

Alyssa shook her head at Emily's mischievous grin. "No, I wouldn't. I was just going to ask if you plan to do any more investigating. I already told you earlier that I wouldn't tell you not to, and I won't. You're a grown woman, and you make your own decisions."

"That I do," Emily said with a bob of her head.

"I'm just worried," Alyssa continued quietly. "I was absolutely terrified when I found out what happened. I care about you very much, and I wouldn't want anything to happen to you."

"Yes, I know. I've already received a bit of a tongue lashing from my son, who seems to think this only proves him right. I see it only as a sign that I need to be a bit more careful. Perhaps I got too bold." She shrugged, ignoring the twinge of pain it caused in her shoulder. "I'll know better for next time."

The young detective looked doubtful. "If you're sure. I do hope you'll forgive me for asking. It's just that I feel a bit responsible, since I've encouraged you so much."

Leaning forward to pat her on the knee, Emily smiled. "My dear, you've helped give this old woman a purpose in life. I love my family, my cat, and my writing. But it's hard when you retire to feel as though you still have some importance . I spent my earlier years getting my education, being a mother, providing for my family. Then I found myself floundering, wondering what I could do that was still meaningful I think this is it, or at least part of it."

"Do you have any other projects in mind?" Alyssa asked. "Or will you wait around for another one to fall in your lap?"

Emily's gaze lifted to a portrait of herself and Sebastian that hung in a frame on the opposite wall. He looked so much like Nathan in that picture, except that he had that sparkling sense of adventure in his eyes. Sebastian was a mild-mannered insurance claims adjuster, not the sort of man who would strike others as being some swashbuckling crusader. Still, she knew he would encourage her if he could be here and knew what she'd been thinking.

But Emily wasn't ready. Not yet. "I'm still thinking about it."

THANK YOU FOR CHOOSING A PUREREAD BOOK!

We hope you enjoyed the story, and as a way to thank you for choosing PureRead we'd like to send you this free Special Edition Cozy, and other fun reader rewards...

Click Here to download your free Cozy Mystery
PureRead.com/cozy

Thanks again for reading.

See you soon!

OTHER BOOKS IN THIS SERIES

If you loved this story and want to follow Emily's antics in other fun easy read mysteries continue **dive straight into other books in this series...**

Read them all...

A Troubling Case Of Murder On The Menu

A Crafty Case Of Murder At The Fair

A Hairy Case of Murder At The Animal Sanctuary

A Clean & Tidy Case of Murder - A Truly Messy Mystery

A Cranky Case of Murder at the Autostore

A Colorful Case of Stolen Art at the Gallery

A Frightful Case of Murder in the Fashion Store

A Beastly Case of Murder at the Bookstore

OUR GIFT TO YOU

AS A WAY TO SAY THANK YOU WE WOULD
LOVE TO SEND YOU THIS SPECIAL EDITION
COZY MYSTERY FREE OF CHARGE.

Our Reader List is 100% FREE

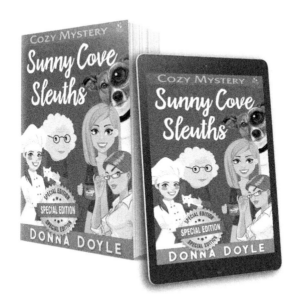

Click Here to download your free Cozy Mystery
PureRead.com/cozy

At PureRead we publish books you can trust. Great tales without smut or swearing, but with all of the mystery and romance you expect from a great story.

Be the first to know when we release new books, take part in our fun competitions, and get surprise free books in your inbox by signing up to our Reader list.

As a thank you you'll receive this exclusive Special Edition Cozy available only to our subscribers...

Click Here to download your free Cozy Mystery
PureRead.com/cozy

Thanks again for reading.
See you soon!

Printed in Great Britain
by Amazon

41787282R20061